妮達和洛奇玩拋擲皮球遊戲。「接住！」她叫道，洛奇跳高，
但是沒有接住球，牠追著球跑出公園，走向馬路去。
「快停！洛奇！快停！」妮達大聲叫，她忙著去抓洛奇竟然看
不到…

Nita was playing ball with Rocky. "Catch!" she shouted. Rocky jumped,
missed and ran after the ball, out of the park and into the road.
"STOP! ROCKY! STOP!" Nita shouted. She was so busy trying to catch
Rocky that she didn't see…

那輛汽車。

the CAR.

那司機大力踏下制動器剎車，啪嚓！但已是太遲了！砰！那輛汽車撞到妮達，她倒下時發出可怕的嘎嚓聲。

The driver slammed on the brakes. SCREECH! But it was too late! THUD! The car hit Nita and she fell to the ground with a sickening CRUNCH.

「妮達！」媽媽大聲尖叫，「請快叫救護車！」她一面叫一面抱著妮達，撫弄著她的頭髮。

那名司機撥電話召喚救護車。

「媽媽，我的腿很痛，」妮達哭著說，大滴的眼淚在她的臉上滾下。

「我知道很痛，但盡量不要動，」媽媽說，「救護車很快便會到。」

"NITA!" Ma screamed. "Someone call an ambulance!" she shouted, stroking Nita's hair and holding her.

The driver dialled for an ambulance.

"Ma, my leg hurts," cried Nita, big tears rolling down her face.

"I know it hurts, but try not to move," said Ma. "Help will be here soon."

救護車來了，兩名醫療人員拿著擔架床走過來。
「你好，我是約翰，你的腿腫得很，它可能折斷了，」他說。
「我將會放上夾板以便阻止腿部移動。」
妮達咬著嘴唇，她的腿實在很痛。
「你真是一個勇敢的女孩，」他一面說一面將妮達躺著的擔架床擡進救護車，媽媽也跟著上了救護車。

The ambulance arrived and two paramedics came with a stretcher.
"Hello, I'm John. Your leg's very swollen. It might be broken," he said. "I'm just going to put these splints on to stop it from moving."
Nita bit her lip. The leg was really hurting.
"You're a brave girl," he said, carrying her gently on the stretcher to the ambulance. Ma climbed in too.

妮達躺在擔架床上，緊握著媽媽。救護車疾駛過街道－警號高鳴，警號燈閃著 － 一直往醫院去。

Nita lay on the stretcher holding tight to Ma, while the ambulance raced through the streets – siren wailing, lights flashing – all the way to the hospital.

在醫院的大門口到處都是人，妮達覺得很害怕。
「哎喲，你發生了什麼事啊？」一位友善的護士問道。
「有一輛汽車撞倒我，我的腿很痛啊，」妮達強忍著眼淚說。
「等醫生看過你之後，我們便給你一些東西止痛，」
他告訴妮達說，「我現在要測探你的體溫和抽取一些血液，
你只會感到少許的針刺。」

At the entrance there were people everywhere. Nita was feeling very scared.
"Oh dear, what's happened to you?" asked a friendly nurse.
"A car hit me and my leg really hurts," said Nita, blinking back the tears.
"We'll give you something for the pain, as soon as the doctor has had a look,"
he told her. "Now I've got to check your temperature and take some blood.
You'll just feel a little jab."

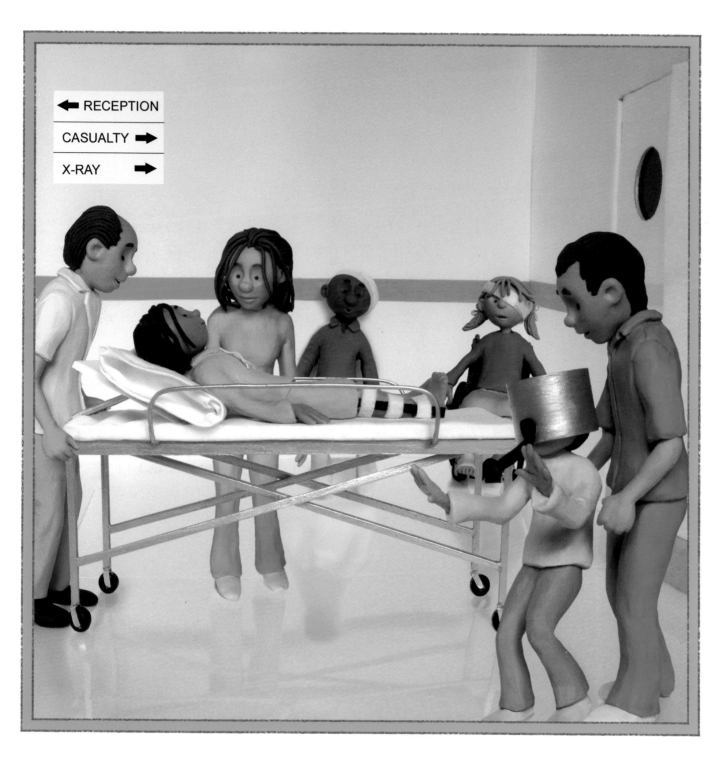

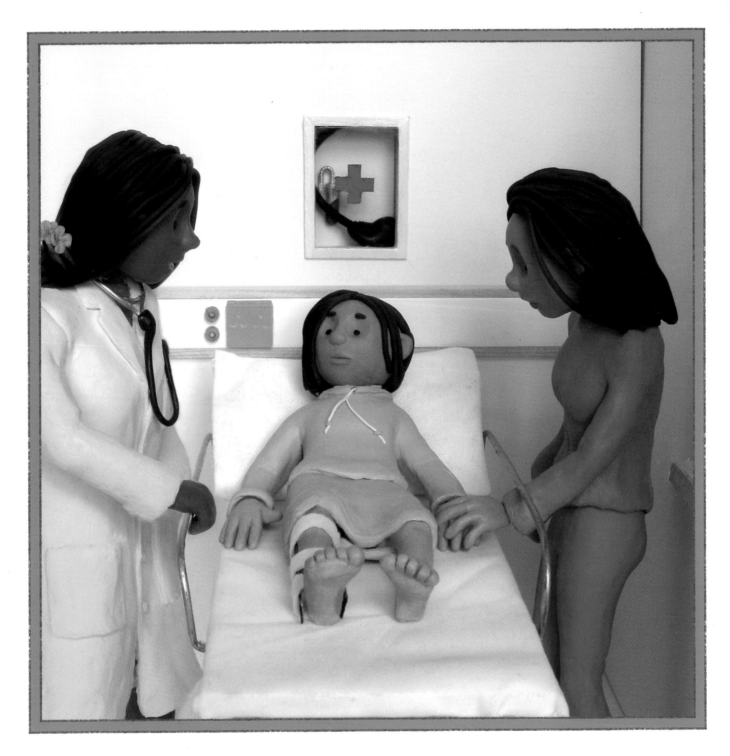

跟著醫生便來了。「你好，妮達，」她說，「哦，
是怎樣發生的？」
「有一輛汽車撞倒我，我的腿很痛啊，」妮達嗚咽著說。
「我會給你一些東西止痛，現在讓我看看你的腿，」醫生說，
「唔，它好像折斷了，我們需要拍 X 光照片，
以便仔細看清楚。」

Next came the doctor. "Hello Nita," she said. "Ooh, how did that happen?"
"A car hit me. My leg really hurts," sobbed Nita.
"I'll give you something to stop the pain. Now let's have a look at your leg," said
the doctor. "Hmm, it seems broken. We'll need an x-ray to take a closer look."

一名友善的護理員把妮達推到 X 光部，那裏有很多人正在等候造 X 光檢查。

最後終於輪到妮達了。「你好，妮達，」X 光攝影師說，「我要用這部機器拍一張你的腿部內側的照片，」她指著 X 光機器說，「不用怕，不會痛的，你只需要在拍 X 光時靜止不動便是了。」

妮達點頭。

A friendly porter wheeled Nita to the x-ray department where lots of people were waiting.

At last it was Nita's turn. "Hello Nita," said the radiographer. "I'm going to take a picture of the inside of your leg with this machine," she said pointing to the x-ray machine. "Don't worry, it won't hurt. You just have to keep very still while I take the x-ray."

Nita nodded.

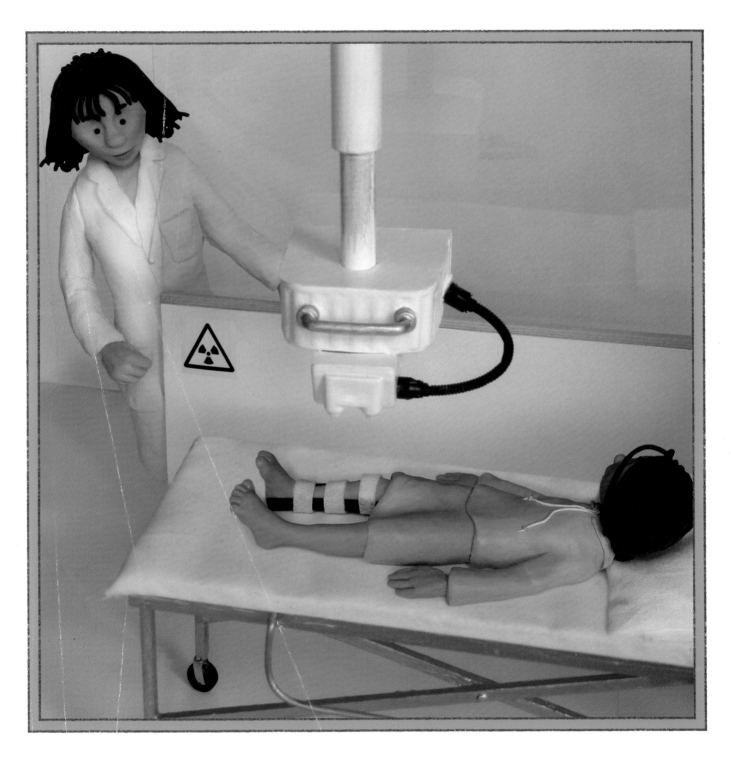

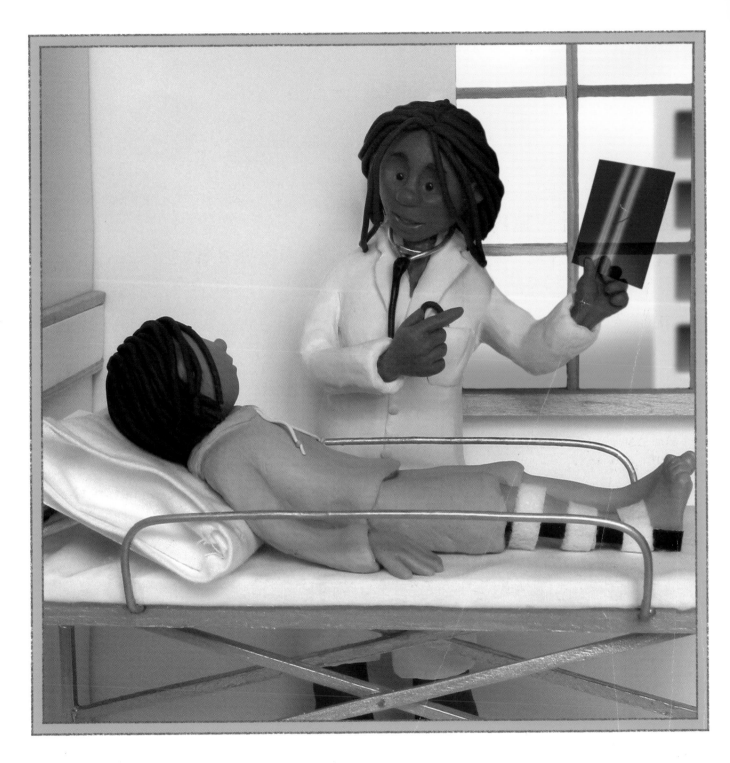

過了一段時間，醫生拿著 X 光照片到來，她將它舉高，
妮達可以看到腿內的腿骨。
「正如我所想的一樣，」醫生說，「你的腿折斷了，
我們需要將它接駁，然後安上石膏繃帶，這樣會將腿部穩固，
讓腿骨接合，但是你的腿現在太腫脹，
你今晚需要留在醫院過一夜。」

A little later the doctor came with the x-ray. She held it up and Nita could see the bone right inside her leg!
"It's as I thought," said the doctor. "Your leg is broken. We'll need to set it and then put on a cast. That'll hold it in place so that the bone can mend. But at the moment your leg is too swollen. You'll have to stay overnight."

護理員將妮達推到兒童病房。「你好，妮達，我叫做露絲，是你的特別護士，我會照顧你， 你來得正好，」她微笑著說。
「爲什麼？」妮達問道。
「因爲現在正好是晚餐時間，我們把你移到床上去，你便可以吃一些食物。」
露絲護士在妮達的腿部周圍放一些冰塊，並給她多一個枕頭，不是用來墊頭的⋯ 而是用來墊腿的。

The porter wheeled Nita to the children's ward. "Hello Nita. My name's Rose and I'm your special nurse. I'll be looking after you. You've come just at the right time," she smiled.
"Why?" asked Nita.
"Because it's dinner time. We'll pop you into bed and then you can have some food."
Nurse Rose put some ice around Nita's leg and gave her an extra pillow, not for her head... but for her leg.

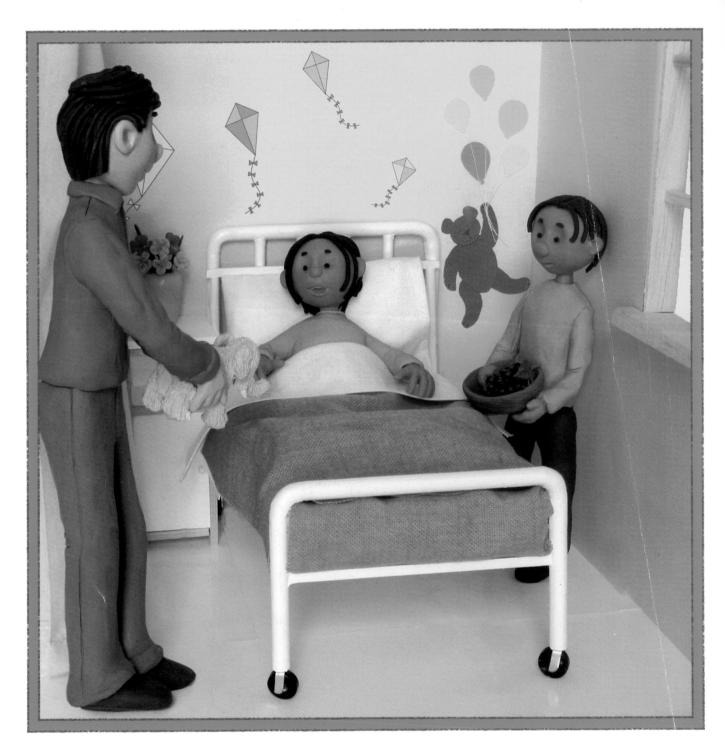

晚飯過後，爸爸和阿志到來，爸爸給妮達一個熱情的擁抱，還把她最喜歡的玩具給她。

「讓我看看你的腿，」阿志說，「啊！很可怕啊，是否很痛？」

「痛得很，」妮達說，「但他們已給我止痛藥。」

露絲護士再次為妮達探測熱度。「現在是時候睡覺了，」她說，「爸爸和你的弟弟要回去，但媽媽可以留下⋯可以留整個晚上。」

After dinner Dad and Jay arrived. Dad gave her a big hug and her favourite toy.

"Let's see your leg?" asked Jay. "Ugh! It's horrible. Does it hurt?"

"Lots," said Nita, "but they gave me pain-killers."

Nurse Rose took Nita's temperature again. "Time to sleep now," she said.

"Dad and your brother will have to go but Ma can stay... all night."

到了第二天早上，醫生檢查妮達的腿。「似乎好多了，」
她說，「我想可以接駁了。」

「那是什麼意思？」妮達問道。

「我們會給你一些麻醉藥，讓你睡覺，然後我們會將腿骨推
到正確的位置，用石膏繃帶穩定它。不用怕，你不會有任何
感覺的，」醫生說。

Early next morning the doctor checked Nita's leg. "Well that looks much better,"
she said. "I think it's ready to be set."

"What does that mean?" asked Nita.

"We're going to give you an anaesthetic to make you sleep. Then we'll push the
bone back in the right position and hold it in place with a cast. Don't worry, you
won't feel a thing," said the doctor.

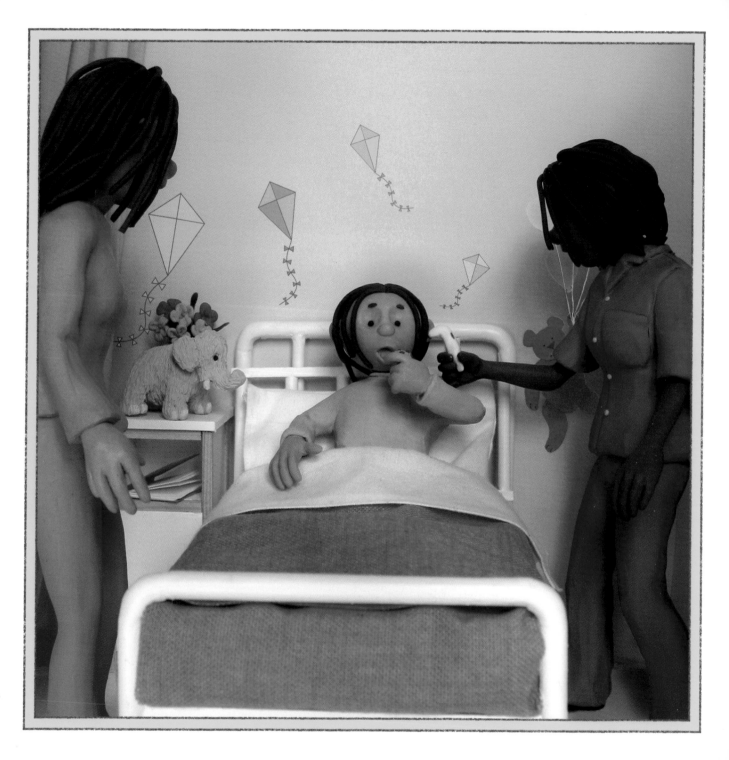

妮達覺得她好像已經睡了一個星期。「媽媽，我睡了多久？」她問道。

「只是一個小時左右，」媽媽說。

「你好，妮達，」露絲護士說，「你睡醒了，真好。你的腿覺得怎麼樣啊？」

「還好，只是感到很重和很僵硬，」妮達說，「可以給我一點東西吃嗎？」

「可以，很快就是午飯時間了，」露絲說。

Nita felt like she'd been asleep for a whole week. "How long have I been sleeping, Ma?" she asked.

"Only about an hour," smiled Ma.

"Hello Nita," said Nurse Rose. "Good to see you've woken up. How's the leg?"

"OK, but it feels so heavy and stiff," said Nita. "Can I have something to eat?"

"Yes, it'll be lunchtime soon," said Rose.

到了午飯時候，妮達已感到好多了，露絲將她移放到輪椅上，讓她能和其他小孩一起。

「你發生了什麼事？」一名男孩問道。

「我的腿折斷了，」妮達說，「你呢？」

「我的耳朵接受了手術，」那男孩說。

By lunchtime Nita was feeling much better. Nurse Rose put her in a wheelchair so that she could join the other children.

"What happened to you?" asked a boy.

"Broke my leg," said Nita. "And you?"

"I had an operation on my ears," said the boy.

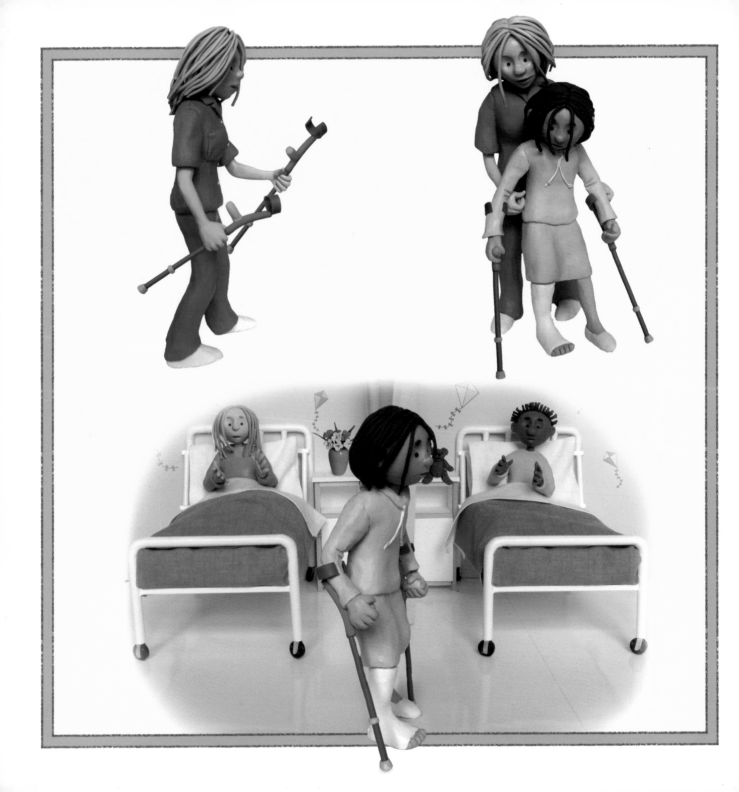

到了下午的時候，物理治療師拿著拐杖到來。「妮達，這東西會協助你走動的，」她說。

妮達跛著、拐著、和扶著，很快便在病房內到處走動。

「很好，」物理治療師說，「我想你已經可以回家了，我去找醫生來看你。」

In the afternoon the physiotherapist came with some crutches. "Here you are Nita. These will help you to get around," she said.

Hobbling and wobbling, pushing and holding, Nita was soon walking around the ward.

"Well done," said the physiotherapist. "I think you're ready to go home. I'll get the doctor to see you."

那天晚上，媽媽、爸爸、阿志和洛奇到醫院來接妮達出院。
「真好啊！」阿志看著妮達的石膏繃帶說，
「我可以在上面繪畫嗎？」
「現在不可以，等我們回家後才可以，」妮達說，
裝上石膏繃帶可能也不是什麼壞事啊！

That evening Ma, Dad, Jay and Rocky came to collect Nita.
"Cool," said Jay seeing Nita's cast. "Can I draw on it?"
"Not now! When we get home," said Nita. Maybe having a
cast wasn't going to be so bad.